THE TALE OF DEVOTION THAT REFUSED TO DIE

ASIF AKHTAR

Contents

Part I – The Spark

    1. The Accidental Love Story I Never Asked For   3

Part II – The Rise

    2. Chanmi: One Word, Infinite Cling   21

Part III – The Storm

    3. The Question That Never Fades   45

Part IV – The Abyss

    4. The Love That Stays, Even When You Don't   61

The Devotion

    5. The Weight Of Unspoken Love   71

The Goodbye Within

    6. The Day I Became A Ghost   85

Final Letter To Her

    7. Tales In Verses   95

These Verses Are Fragments Of A Heart Torn Between Hope And Despair. Yet, Life Moves Forward, As Do I, Even If My Words Are Left Unspoken.

The Last Page, but Not the End   119

Part I – The Spark

"Chanmi"

The name you gave, still echoes soft,
A whisper in my storm.
A word so small, yet all I crave,
My universe in form.

You said it once, then locked it tight,
Like stars you never chase.
But I still wear it every night,
A smile upon my face.

CHAPTER ONE

THE ACCIDENTAL LOVE STORY I NEVER ASKED FOR

The Uninvited Guest Called Love

They never warn you about love. Not really. People talk about it like it's this grand, magical thing—like a scene straight out of a movie where everything falls into place, and life suddenly makes sense. But that's a lie. A big, ridiculous lie. Love isn't gentle. It doesn't knock politely on your heart and wait to be let in. No, love kicks the door down, barges in like an uninvited guest, and starts wrecking the place.

One day, you're just a normal person, minding your own business, living your perfectly manageable life. And the next? You're a disaster. A full-blown emotional catastrophe. You start tripping over air, forgetting how words work, and replaying every tiny interaction like a detective trying to crack a case. Except the only mystery is: Why her?

Why did my heart decide to latch onto the one person who probably doesn't even know I exist? And why, despite knowing how ridiculous this all is, can't I stop myself from falling deeper? It's like my emotions handed over the controls to some reckless, love-drunk version of myself, and now I'm stuck riding this rollercoaster with no seatbelt.

The worst part? Love doesn't even give you time to prepare. It doesn't build up slowly or give you a fair warning. It hits you like a freight train out of nowhere. One second, you're fine, and the next, your heart is sprinting like it's late for a meeting. You start noticing things you never noticed before—like the way she laughs, or how her eyes catch the light, or how she tucks her hair behind her ear when she's thinking. And suddenly, those tiny, insignificant moments become the most important things in the universe.

I wish I could say I handled it well. That I played it cool and effortlessly navigated this whole "falling in love" thing. But the truth? I crashed and burned. I fumbled my way through every conversation, turned into a malfunctioning robot every time she was near, and single-handedly made my life ten times more complicated.
And yet... I couldn't stop.

This is the story of how love grabbed me by the collar, shook me senseless, and left me in a constant state of emotional chaos. It's messy, awkward, and honestly kind of humiliating. But if you're ready to witness a trainwreck in real time, buckle up.

Because this? This is just the beginning.

Part 1: A Rollercoaster of Realizations

Love, they say, sneaks up on you like a thief in the night. But let's be real—love doesn't sneak. It doesn't gently tap you on the shoulder and wait for you to notice. No, it barges in, uninvited, and wrecks your life in the most beautifully chaotic way possible. One minute, you're cruising through your regular life, perfectly content, and the next, you're head over heels for someone you never saw coming. It's like a sudden tornado on a perfectly clear day. I never signed up for this. But here I am, falling into it anyway, and I think it's too late to turn back now.

The First Glance That Changed Everything

It all started when I saw her for the first time. I didn't know it was her then. I didn't know she was about to change my world. I was just standing there, minding my own business, doing whatever it is that I do in class, when—there she was.

She wasn't trying to stand out, and that's exactly what made her so captivating. She wasn't the loudest in the room. She wasn't the one with the most attention-grabbing outfit. No, she was just... there. And that was enough. She stood near the classroom window, laughing with her friends. Her laughter wasn't like any other I had heard. It was the kind of laughter that fills the air and makes everything feel lighter. It was as if she didn't just laugh; she made everything around her laugh too. And her smile? Let's not even go there. It wasn't just a smile—it was a moment. A fleeting, perfect moment where time seemed to stand still.

I stood there, frozen, staring at her like an idiot. Not even realizing how much my world had just shifted.

In that one instant, I realized something important. I had a huge problem. My heart was already racing. And I had absolutely no idea why. But there was something in the way she smiled, in the way she moved, in the way the sunlight seemed to love her more than anyone else. And I couldn't look away. I couldn't even try to.

The Traitor Known as My Brain

And then my brain—my supposed "best friend"—decided to betray me. It had always been reliable before. But no. The moment she stepped into my world, it decided to go on vacation. My brain couldn't handle the complexity of it all. One second, I was a normal guy, just doing normal things. And the next second, I was having thoughts I'd never experienced before.

What just happened? Why is my heart beating like a drum? Is this supposed to feel this overwhelming? Why am I acting like a complete idiot?

It was like my brain was firing on all cylinders, but none of them were the right ones. I kept trying to figure it out. I kept thinking, Is this love? But no, it wasn't just love—it was a mess. A chaotic, unfiltered, unpredictable mess.

The Awkward Attempts at Acting Normal

If you've ever tried to act normal around someone you like, you know how much of a disaster it can be. I like to think of myself as someone who can keep things cool. After all, I'm not a walking disaster—at least, I wasn't before she came along.

But here I am, trying to act normal whenever she's around. And of course, I fail spectacularly.

There was this one time. She walked past me in the hallway. Simple, right? No big deal. But my reaction? I tripped. Over absolutely nothing. It was as if the ground itself decided to conspire against me. I stumbled forward, managing to grab the side of the wall, but still feeling like I had just performed an Olympic-level face-plant.

She glanced at me as I awkwardly straightened up, and all I could think was: Did she see that? Did she just see me trip in front of her?
Let's just say I'm pretty sure she didn't see it. Or maybe she did. Either way, it was a tragedy.

The Water Cooler Chronicles

Let's talk about the "casual" run-ins, shall we? Because there's nothing "casual" about them when you've mentally rehearsed them 50 times in your head. Case in point: the water cooler.

I had a brilliant plan. I would casually walk up to the water cooler, grab a drink, and hopefully make a smooth comment about how hot the weather was. Casual, right? I even practiced in front of the mirror.

Well, guess what? My plan failed before I even got started. She walked up to the water cooler first. Of course, she did. My brain went into panic mode. I stood there, holding an empty water bottle, staring at her like I had forgotten how to function. She smiled politely, filling up her bottle, and I did... nothing.

Well, I did try to make conversation. But it came out as a weird, awkward string of words that I think were supposed to be something coherent but ended up sounding like a malfunctioning robot. "Hi... um, hot... uh, weather?" It was the worst. The absolute worst.

Group Projects and Other Nightmare Scenarios

Nothing is more terrifying than a group project when the person you like is in your group. It's like suddenly, everyone expects you to be smart and articulate, and you're just there sweating bullets.

She was sitting across from me during our project. I tried to focus on the task at hand—something to do with science, which should have been easy—but all I could focus on was the fact that she was right there.

You would think passing a simple piece of paper would be easy, but no. My hand was shaking so much that I thought I might drop it before it reached her. When I finally handed it over, I swear I could see her look at me with concern.

Was it pity? I wasn't sure.

She asked me if I was okay. And of course, I lied. "Yeah, I'm fine, just, uh, cold." It was 30°C outside. There was no reason to be cold. But my brain decided it wasn't going to help me that day.

The Little Things That Drive You Crazy

You don't notice the little things in life until they start driving you insane.

Like, have you ever noticed the way someone tucks their hair behind their ear when they're focused? Or how they absentmindedly doodle on their notebook when they're bored? I could watch her do that for hours and still not be bored.

And the funny part? She didn't even know. To her, it was just a normal day. To me? It was everything.

I couldn't help but memorize the way she moved. The way she smiled. Every little detail stuck with me like a song on repeat. I could've told you what kind of pen she used, how she chewed the edge of her pencil when thinking, and what color her shoes were on any given day.

Why, Man, Why?

It's funny. When you're in love—or whatever this feeling is—it doesn't make sense. Why her? Of all the people in the world, why did I get stuck on her?

Maybe it's her smile. Maybe it's the way she lights up when she talks about her favorite things. Maybe it's her laugh. God, her laugh. It's like music, and it's stuck in my head on a loop.

But no matter how much I try to rationalize it, I can't. There's something deeper, something I can't explain. And I don't think I ever will.

I sit here, trying to make sense of it, asking myself the same question over and over: Why, man, why? Why did this happen to me?

The Quiet Chaos

She doesn't know. And that's the worst part. She goes through her life, completely unaware of the storm she's caused in mine. She's laughing, talking, doing her thing, while I'm here—silent, caught in this web of unspoken words.

And there have been moments, tiny moments, when our worlds collided. The time she borrowed my pen, for example. I handed it to her with what I hoped was a smooth, casual grin. But inside, I was screaming, Take the pen, take my heart, take whatever you want.

The Struggle of Just Saying Hi

One of the hardest things about liking someone from afar is getting up the courage to say even the simplest things. "Hi." That's it. Two letters, one syllable, and yet it felt like it would take all the strength I had to say it without stammering.

But I did it. I don't remember the exact moment, but I do remember my heart pounding in my chest. She smiled, said "Hi" back, and that was it. But I could've sworn time stopped in that one moment.

The Daydreamer's Curse

I couldn't help but daydream about what could be. Maybe we would talk more. Maybe she would notice me. Maybe she'd realize that I was actually kind of interesting, deep down. The possibility of anything happening felt as distant as a shooting star. But still, I couldn't help myself. I dreamed about it.

The trouble with daydreaming is that you end up overthinking everything. How would I talk to her? What if she didn't like me back? What if I made things awkward? My mind would run through a million scenarios, each one worse than the last.

The Longing That Never Fades

But despite the self-doubt, despite the awkwardness, despite the pain of knowing she might never feel the same way, I couldn't stop. And I think that's the worst part of this whole thing: the way this love, unrequited as it may be, never fades. It's like it lives inside you, quietly, endlessly.

Why, Man, Why?

It's funny, isn't it? How life throws things at you that you never asked for. I didn't ask for this. I didn't want it. But somehow, here I am, trying to make sense of a feeling that doesn't need to be explained.

And I don't think it's something I'll ever be able to put into words—not truly. Because no matter how much I try, there's always more. So much more to say.

Part 2: The Awkwardness, the Texting, and the Silence

Alright, let's talk about this whole texting situation. Picture this: We're not in the same class. She's in 9th grade, and I'm stuck in 10th, two ships passing in the night, or in this case, two souls separated by a hallway and endless awkward encounters. The only connection we have is... WhatsApp. Oh, WhatsApp—where people say so much without saying anything at all.

Here's the thing: I text first. Always. Why? I have no idea. It's like some twisted version of playing the hero in my own emotional soap opera. She's probably got better things to do—like, I don't know, saving the world from the impending doom of algebra—but me? I'm sitting here, tapping away, sending her a message like it's the most normal thing in the world.

The Great Texting Adventures

You know how it goes, right? The excitement when you send that first message: Will she reply? Will she actually care about what I have to say? But the real fun begins when you get that one-liner response. You know the one I'm talking about: the "Okay," the "Lol," or—if I'm lucky—a "Yes, I'm free."

Every message feels like I'm reading a novel where the plot is entirely up to me to interpret. Every dot, every "K," every "Hmm" gets analyzed to death. Is she being short because she's busy? Or is this the sign of the world's most painful rejection?

Sometimes, I feel like I'm speaking into the void. I send a message, and then I wait. And wait. And wait. Checking my phone every five minutes like it's some kind of live news feed. And then, when she does reply? Oh, the joy! I get that little thrill—like I just scored the winning goal in a soccer match I didn't even know I was playing. But what's worse than getting a response? Not getting one.

The Curse of the Left on Read

There's a special kind of heartbreak that comes from being "left on read." It's like a cruel joke. You send your message, you see that tiny blue double check mark, and you wait. And wait. And wait. You refresh the app as though you're checking for the latest breaking news, only to be greeted by... nothing. Absolute radio silence.

And then you wonder: "Is she busy? Or does she not want to talk to me?" Wait, did I say something weird? Now I'm spiraling into existential chaos. It's like trying to decipher the meaning of life through emojis. You laugh, but you know it's real. Every time she replies, I find myself fighting off the instinct to overanalyze, to wonder if I'm reading too much into things.

It's all fun and games until your mind starts creating

scenarios. You tell yourself, "Oh, it's nothing," but deep down, you know your heart is doing somersaults in your chest every time the typing dots appear. If only I could not feel like a teenager texting in a movie. But no, I'm pretty sure I'm an extra in some badly-scripted teen drama.

The Awkward Texting Marathon

So, we talk on WhatsApp. Great. But it's not like she's texting me first. That would be too easy, right? No, I'm the one starting every conversation. Every. Single. One. It's like a one-sided ping-pong match where I'm the only one trying to hit the ball back.

Let's be real here. I've tried everything. I've tried starting with a simple "Hey, how's it going?" But that only ever leads to the dreaded "Fine" reply. So, I get creative. I start asking about her day, her classes, her plans. Anything to get more than one-word answers. Sometimes I'll throw in a joke, maybe something from the meme vault, hoping that will spark a conversation. And sometimes—just sometimes—it works. But more often than not, it doesn't.

Here's the kicker: when she does answer, it's like she's doing me a huge favor. "Yeah, I was busy with school," she'll say. And I'm over here like, "Yeah, me too. I only had an existential crisis in geometry class, no big deal."

But then, when I finally manage to get a conversation going, it's like a rollercoaster ride of emotional highs and lows. One second, we're laughing about something silly, and the next, there's silence. And I'm left wondering if I've crossed some invisible line, if my humor was just too much, if I've ruined everything in one message.

The Eternal Hope of a Face-to-Face Conversation

There's something magical about imagining the possibility of talking to her in real life. I mean, sure, we're in different classes, but occasionally our paths cross in the hallways. Those brief moments, when our eyes meet, it's like the universe pauses for a split second. I could just say something, anything, and maybe start a real conversation. But no. I freeze up. Every. Single. Time.

And when I see her talking to someone else? Ouch. It's like a gut punch to the soul. I know I shouldn't care. I mean, why should I? But still, it stings. Here I am, barely able to string together a sentence, and there she is, laughing and talking effortlessly with someone else. And the worst part? She probably doesn't even know how badly my heart is performing backflips in my chest just from seeing her.

And then, just when I think I've reached the peak of awkwardness, it happens. The ultimate "accidental" meeting. You know, the one where I see her and then immediately make some poor decision that I'll replay in my mind for the next 48 hours. I've done it all—the awkward wave, the weird "Hey" that comes out way too loud, the "I'm just casually standing here" stance. It's all part of the repertoire of embarrassing moments I've collected over time.

The Emotional Confusion

Sometimes, I wonder if I'm the only one who feels like this.

Is this what everyone else goes through when they're in love? Or is it just me, overthinking everything, creating this tangled web of emotions that I can't untangle?

Why is it that love has this magical way of making you question your worth? I've had moments where I just want to scream, "What's wrong with me?" I see her being so natural, so comfortable in her own skin, and I wonder, Why can't I be that way? It's like I'm constantly trying to measure up to some ideal I've created in my head, but the truth is, I'm just trying to keep it together.

But then, there's that part of me that refuses to give up. It's the part that keeps texting first, that keeps trying to make her laugh, to share a joke, to make her see me as someone she can talk to. Because, deep down, I know that if I stop trying, if I stop texting, if I stop making the effort, that's it. Game over. The chance to be a part of her life will slip through my fingers, and I'll be left wondering what could have been.

The Silence and the Question: Why, Man, Why?

And now, as I sit here, reflecting on it all, I'm left with one simple question: Why, man, why? Why do I keep putting myself through this emotional rollercoaster? Why do I keep hoping that something will change? Maybe it's because, deep down, I believe in the possibility of something more. Maybe I believe that if I keep trying, she'll notice me—really notice me—and everything will change.

But for now, I'll keep texting. I'll keep waiting. I'll keep wondering if maybe, just maybe, I'm not the only one who

feels something.
And so, the chapter ends here. Or does it?

Falling in love is easy. Saying more than 'Hi'? That's the
real challenge.

Whispers of a Silent Heart

I saw you once, just passing by,
Noticed the sparkle in your eye.
A second's glance, that's all it took,
And suddenly I was hooked.
Your smile was bright, like morning light,
But I just stood there, out of sight.
Trying to act cool, trying to be sly,
But all I did was mumble, "Hi."
You laughed out loud, a melody so sweet,
And for a moment, my heart skipped a beat.
But did you hear? Did you even know?
Or was I just another face in the row?
I watch from afar, oh what a sight,
Trying to figure out if this feels right.
Should I speak? Should I say something more?
But every time I try, I just stare at the floor.
It's like I'm stuck in a never-ending game,
Wanting to speak, but fearing the same.
What if I trip over my own feet?
What if I stutter and look like a cheat?
You're always there, just out of reach,
A mystery I'll never quite breach.
I imagine us talking, laughing, too,
But in reality, I'm still stuck on "Hi" and "How do you do?"
Sometimes I wonder what you'd say,
If you knew how I felt today.

Would you smile, or would you run?
Would you laugh and say, "This is fun!"
But instead, I'll stay in my little shell,
Hoping you notice, but never tell.
For now, I'll just be the silent guy,
Who wonders if you see me, and wonders why.
So here I am, caught in suspense,
Trying to figure out what makes sense.
Should I step up, or stay behind?
A silent love, a tangled mind.
Will you notice, or am I too late?
Is this love? Or just my fate?
Maybe one day, I'll find the nerve,
Until then, I'll just observe.
But if you see me trip again,
Laugh it off, it's not the end.
For in this awkward, silly mess,
Maybe one day, I'll confess.

Part II – The Rise

"Penguin"

Not just a name, a world I knew,
Wrapped in kindness, bathed in hue.
You taught me love without a word,
A silent prayer, never heard.

You called me friend, I called you mine,
Between each joke, a hidden sign.
You held the sun, I held the shade—
But smiled, just so you stayed.

CHAPTER TWO

CHANMI: ONE WORD, INFINITE CLING

Introduction :

Alright, here's the deal. This is the story of a guy (me, of course) who tried his best to carve a little spot in her heart. Spoiler alert: it didn't exactly go as planned. But hey, at least it's good for a laugh, so let's dive into the tale of Chanmi—the one word that rocked my world for exactly one glorious moment.

You see, I had this brilliant idea: "What if I get her to give me a nickname? Something special, something only she calls me. A little piece of me that's just ours." Genius, right? Well, turns out, asking someone for a nickname is like asking them to give you the secret to the universe—kind of awkward and totally unrequested.

But I wasn't backing down. I worked up the nerve, cornered

her one day (figuratively, not literally—I'm not a stalker), flashed my most charming "I'm harmless, I swear" smile, and casually asked, "Can you call me something? Just once? Something only you'll call me?"

She hesitated. I could see her brain running a quick assessment: "Is this guy crazy, or just lonely?" But then, in what felt like a divine moment, she said it. Chanmi.

BOOM. That was it. Fireworks. I swear, my soul took a little vacation. It wasn't just a word—it was THE word. The word that felt like it was written in the stars. I looked at her with awe, thinking, "Did she just say that?!" She did. And for a glorious second, I was the happiest fool alive.

But here's where the humor (and the pain) kicks in. She. Never. Said. It. Again. Yeah, you heard me right. One and done. Like a limited-edition item, Chanmi was a one-time offer. And me? I held onto that single word like it was the last cookie in the jar, hoping, praying that she'd just slip it into a conversation one more time. Spoiler alert: she didn't.

And of course, I tried. Oh, I tried. I'd casually bring it up, like, "Remember when you called me Chanmi? That was nice, right? You could... you know... say it again?" Her response? A smile. No word. Just a smile. And not the "aww, cute" smile. More like the "Oh no, here he goes again" smile.

And here comes the painful bit (because what's humor without a little heartache?): she probably didn't even remember it. For her, it was just a passing thing. A throwaway moment. For me, though? It was everything. I turned that one word into a lifeline, a badge of honor, and a painful reminder of how far I'll go to hold on to something that doesn't belong to me.

But here's the thing—Chanmi was never just a nickname. It was a word that only sounded right when it came from her lips. It was like it was made for her voice, and only her voice. It didn't just mean "me"; it meant her and me. And that's something no one else could ever replace. It was ours... even if it was for just a second.

Yeah, I'm being ridiculous. I begged for it, clung to it, turned it into something bigger than it ever needed to be. But that's love, isn't it? It turns little things into everything. And sometimes, it turns you into a certified fool, too.

So here I am, the self-proclaimed Chanmi enthusiast, still holding onto a word that doesn't exist in her world anymore. She's out there living her life, laughing at memes, while I'm here reminiscing about the one time she called me that name. The one time that felt like everything.

And, you know what? That's okay. I've learned to accept it. She's not mine, never was, and probably never will be. She's someone else's, and that one moment—when she called me Chanmi—that's mine. It's my little treasure, my secret, my one silly memory.

And maybe, just maybe, one day she'll remember it. Maybe she won't. Either way, it doesn't matter. Because in the end, I'll still be Chanmi. The guy who got one word, but held onto it forever.
So yeah, I'm probably the only person who can say they're

laughing at their own heartbreak. But that's the beauty of it, isn't it? The cling of a word, the laugh through the pain, and the hope that maybe, just maybe, someone will remember us in their own special way.

And who knows? Maybe one day, she'll call me Chanmi again. Or maybe I'll just keep calling myself that. It's not like anyone's listening anyway...
Ughhhh Let's begin the chapter

Part 1: Born in a Moment, Buried in Silence

It all started with a name. A single word that, for reasons I couldn't quite understand at the time, became the center of my world. Chanmi.

Now, names are usually just labels. They're how we identify people, nothing more than sounds strung together to make sense in a world full of chaos. And yet, there was something about Chanmi that transcended its usual function. It wasn't just a name. It wasn't just a label. It felt... special.

I'd heard it before, countless times. Her name, the one that hung in the air every time she spoke to someone, the one I never paid much attention to because, well, it was just another name. At least, that's what I thought. But the moment she said it to me, in that quiet, fleeting moment in the hallway, everything changed.

It wasn't a big deal to her, I'm sure of it. She said it casually, like she had said it to dozens of other people before. But to me? That one simple word held all the meaning in the world. It felt like a whisper in a sea of noise. I could almost hear the music behind it, the way the word floated between us, making me feel like there was something deeper hidden in that brief exchange.

She probably didn't even notice, but I did. I noticed everything. The way she said it, the way it rolled off her tongue, the way her eyes met mine for just a second before she turned away. For me, that one instant was enough to make me feel like I was floating, like the world had stopped moving just long enough for us to connect.

Of course, I wasn't naïve enough to believe that she meant anything by it. To her, it was just another friendly, passing exchange. But to me? That was the moment when my world tilted, when everything I thought I knew about myself started to unravel.

I found myself replaying it over and over in my mind. Chanmi. The name. The sound. The way she spoke it. It was like an echo that wouldn't fade, and it followed me everywhere. I heard it in the quiet moments, in the hum of the classroom, in the soft rustle of pages turning, in the buzz of voices around me. It was always there, lingering in the background, growing louder each time I thought about it.

And soon, I was obsessed.
Not just with her, but with that one word.
That one word that had somehow managed to wrap itself around my thoughts and twisted into something far bigger than it had any right to be.
Every time I heard her voice, I'd hold my breath, waiting

for her to say it again.
Chanmi.
But it didn't come.
Not like I hoped.
Not like I imagined.

Instead, I found myself waiting for every little interaction, every brief moment we shared, hoping it would lead to her speaking my name again. I'd walk down the hallways, pretending to be busy with my phone, all the while scanning the crowd for any sign of her. I'd stand by my locker, doing my best to look casual, hoping that somehow, she'd wander over and say something—anything—that would lead to her calling me Chanmi again.

And when it didn't happen, I'd go over it in my mind. What did I do wrong? Was I not standing in the right spot? Did I not give her the right look? Why wasn't she saying it again? It became this cycle—this endless loop of waiting, hoping, doubting myself, questioning everything. But the more I waited, the more frustrated I became.

That's when I started to notice it. The way I was acting. The way my thoughts had started to consume me. I wasn't just thinking about her anymore. I was thinking about her name. Chanmi. I had taken this tiny little interaction, this casual moment, and turned it into something that defined my entire day. It wasn't healthy. It wasn't even normal. But I couldn't help it.

So, there I was, caught in this whirlpool of my own making, unable to break free. Every time I saw her, I'd feel this surge of hope, this brief flicker of excitement, only to have it fade the moment she passed me by without so much as a glance. And yet, despite all the rejection, despite the silent moments where I stood there, invisible and unnoticed, I couldn't let go. I couldn't stop thinking about her, about her name.

I would tell myself that it didn't matter. That it was just a name, just a passing word that had no real meaning. But deep down, I knew it was more than that. It had become this symbol—this tiny glimmer of something that I clung to with all my might, hoping that one day, it would turn into something more.

And that's when the realization hit me. One day, I woke up and asked myself: What am I doing? What was I really waiting for? Was I just hoping that some cosmic force would intervene and make her notice me? Was I expecting her to see something in me that I couldn't even see myself?

I realized that I had turned a small moment into this monumental event in my mind. That simple word, Chanmi, had become this unattainable goal, a far-off dream that I kept running toward, only to have it slip through my fingers every time.

In the quiet moments when I wasn't obsessing over her, I started to laugh at myself. How had I gotten so caught up in this? It wasn't even about her anymore—it was about the idea of her. The idea of something that would never be.

But here's the thing: it wasn't all bad. Sure, it was ridiculous. Sure, it was embarrassing. But there was something beautiful about the way my heart had invested itself in a single word, in a single moment. It was a reminder of how fragile we are, how easy it is to get lost in something that doesn't exist. But at the same time, it was a reminder of how deeply we can feel, how powerful even the smallest things can be.

So, I decided to let go. Not because I didn't care about Chanmi—I still did. But because I had to let go of the fantasy. I had to stop holding onto something that wasn't real.

And while I knew it was time to move on, there would always be a small part of me that carried that moment with me. A small part of me that would always remember Chanmi, not as a symbol of unrequited love, but as a reminder of how deeply a single word can change everything.

After all, sometimes the things that never happen are the ones that shape us the most.

The process of letting go was slow. I couldn't just flick a switch and stop thinking about her. But every day, little by little, I started to move on. I started to find peace in the chaos, to laugh at myself for the way I had turned a name into a dream.

And as time passed, I found myself learning something I didn't expect. That maybe, just maybe, the beauty of the moment wasn't in the outcome. Maybe the beauty was in the feeling itself—in the way something so simple could make you feel alive.

So, here I am, moving forward. Still carrying the memory

of Chanmi, but with a little more clarity, a little more perspective. I don't know what the future holds, but I'm okay with that. Sometimes, the best things come when you stop looking for them.

The days that followed that fleeting exchange in the hallway were like a blur of confusion and hope. Chanmi. That word echoed in my mind like a song stuck on repeat. I would hear it in the hustle and bustle of school corridors, in the quiet moments when I was left to my thoughts, and sometimes, even in my dreams. It was like a melody that refused to fade, always lingering in the background of my mind.

I would catch myself lost in thought during class, staring at my notebook, my pencil frozen in mid-air, as the name floated before me like a whisper. My friends noticed it. "Hey, what's up with you lately?" they'd ask, tapping me on the shoulder.

"Nothing," I'd reply with a grin, trying to cover up the storm of emotions churning within me. But deep down, I knew they could see through my act. They knew me well enough to spot when something was off.

At first, I thought I could shrug it off. I thought, "It's just a name. Just a word. I'll move on. It doesn't mean anything." But as much as I tried to tell myself that, my heart didn't seem to get the message. Every time I saw her in the hallway or heard her laugh across the room, that same weight would drop in my chest. The weight of unspoken words, of what could have been, of what might never be.

I began to realize that it wasn't just the name that was

holding me captive. It was everything around it. The sound of her voice, the way her eyes twinkled when she was excited, the way she moved so gracefully through the crowd like she belonged in a different world. I didn't just want to hear her name again; I wanted everything. I wanted to be the one to make her laugh, to share a quiet moment with her, to be someone she looked at and thought, Yeah, he's worth it.

But those moments never came. Instead, there I was, sitting in the cafeteria, my tray of food untouched, watching her laugh with someone else. And the worst part? I couldn't look away. Every time she laughed, every time she spoke, every time she smiled, I felt like I was being pulled deeper into this world of longing I didn't know how to escape.

And the more I tried to escape, the harder it became. My friends noticed I was quieter, more distant. At first, they teased me about it, asking if I was falling for someone. I would laugh it off, trying to act like I didn't care. But deep inside, I was hoping that one day, just one day, I would be the one she would look at with that same warmth, the one she would call out to with the same affection she showed to everyone else.
But that wasn't happening.

Instead, I was stuck in this weird limbo, this space between hope and reality, where every glance, every casual "hello," felt like it meant something more. And I wasn't sure how to handle it. I wanted to reach out to her, to make a connection, but the more I tried, the more I realized that she wasn't even looking in my direction.

It was then that I had to confront something uncomfortable: I had built up this entire scenario in my mind.

It wasn't her that was keeping me stuck; it was the idea of her. The idea of what could be. I was falling in love with the image of her in my head, not the person she actually was. And that was a hard pill to swallow.

There's something about unrequited love that does something strange to you. It warps your sense of reality. You begin to see signs everywhere. A smile. A glance. The way her hair catches the light. You start to convince yourself that every little detail is a message, a sign, a clue that maybe, just maybe, she feels something for you too.

But the truth is, I was just creating stories in my mind. She wasn't giving me any of these signs. They were all in my head. And that's when I realized: I wasn't just in love with her. I was in love with the fantasy of her. The fantasy that I had built up around a name.

That's when I decided to step back. It wasn't easy. In fact, it felt like I was walking away from a dream, from something that had felt so real to me. But the more I thought about it, the more I realized that real love didn't come from fantasies. It came from connections, from shared experiences, from truly seeing someone for who they are, not just who you imagine them to be.

So, I did what I had to do: I started letting go.

It wasn't a dramatic moment. It wasn't like I stood up and announced to the world, "I'm done!" No. It was quieter than that. It was small moments of clarity—moments where I stopped hoping for a glance, moments where I chose to focus on other things, moments where I allowed myself to breathe without carrying the weight of that unspoken love.

But letting go didn't mean forgetting. It didn't mean erasing the memory of Chanmi. No, it meant accepting that some things aren't meant to be. It meant allowing myself the space to feel that loss without letting it consume me. It meant recognizing that the feelings I had were real, but that sometimes, real love wasn't enough.

And as I let go, something unexpected happened. I started to notice other things. Little things. Like how my friends made me laugh when I needed it most, or how my favorite song sounded just a little sweeter when I wasn't so consumed with longing.

I began to realize that life wasn't all about waiting for a moment that may never come. Life was about living in the here and now, about finding joy in the present, no matter how small.

That's when I truly started to smile again. Not because I had moved on from Chanmi, but because I had found a little bit of peace within myself. I had found the ability to appreciate the beauty of the world without needing it to revolve around a single name.

It was a slow process, but with each passing day, I found myself standing a little taller, breathing a little easier.

And when I saw her again—Chanmi, walking through the hallways, laughing with her friends—something shifted inside me. I didn't feel the rush of emotions anymore. I didn't feel the ache in my chest.

I just smiled.

I didn't need anything from her anymore. I was finally free.

And in that freedom, I found something beautiful. Something unexpected. The realization that love, at its core, isn't about possession or ownership. It's about appreciation. It's about letting go of the fantasy and accepting the reality. It's about smiling at the person you love, even from a distance, and knowing that their happiness doesn't depend on you.

I had been holding on to Chanmi for so long, thinking that she was the key to my happiness. But the truth was, I had always had the key inside me.

And now, I had the freedom to unlock the door to my own heart.

Part 2: The Seven Stages of Love

After that unforgettable moment, where time froze and everything seemed like a surreal dream—I realized something that hit me like a ton of bricks: I hadn't moved on. Nope. Not at all. Not even a little bit. Here I was, still clinging to those fleeting moments, still replaying them in my head like they were the highlight reel of my life. It was like I was stuck in the past, and the future? Well, it was just some abstract concept I didn't want to face.

But this, this was the harsh truth. I hadn't moved on. And the universe had a funny way of making sure I realized it. And so, I decided to take a step back and look at what was going on with me. I wasn't just stuck in some endless loop of unrequited feelings; no, I had entered the magical, painful, and oh-so-confusing world of the seven stages of love.

Buckle up, because this is going to be a bumpy ride.

Stage 1: Infatuation.

This is where everything started. I'm talking full-on, heart-skipping-a-beat, butterflies-in-my-stomach infatuation. It wasn't just liking her, oh no. It was beyond that. I was practically a human version of a teenage fangirl at a concert. Every time she said my name, I felt like I'd just won the lottery. I would replay it in my head over and over again.

I remember sitting in class one day, trying to focus on the lesson, but all I could think about was that one time she looked at me, smiled, and said, "Hey, Chanmi." I swear, if my heart had a volume knob, it would've been on full blast. It was like hearing your favorite song on the radio after a bad day—suddenly, everything made sense.

And of course, I began to overanalyze everything. I'd start texting myself: "Is she thinking about me too? Does she look at me the way I look at her?" And let's be honest, I'd craft entire imaginary conversations in my head. I was basically writing an Oscar-winning script, and I was the lead actor. "Wow, Chanmi, you're so cool. How do you stay so calm?" "Oh, it's nothing. I just pretend to have my life together." Cue dramatic music.

But of course, the reality? I was a nervous wreck every time she even acknowledged my existence. The truth was that I couldn't even get through a simple conversation without making myself look like a confused penguin at a fashion show.

Stage 2: Denial.

At this stage, I was like the kid who denies they ate all the cookies, even though their face is covered in chocolate. "I'm fine. This is fine. I don't care. It's not like I'm obsessed or anything. I'm perfectly normal." I had to keep telling myself that over and over. Denial was my defense mechanism—my way of pretending this was all just a "harmless crush." Yeah, sure, a "harmless crush" that made me feel like I was going to explode every time she walked past me.

But denial couldn't last forever. There's only so long you can pretend that you're not waiting by the phone for that one magical text that you know will never come. You start making excuses: "Oh, she's probably just busy," or "Maybe she's not into texting much." Meanwhile, I'm staring at my phone like a lost puppy. The longer I stayed in denial, the more ridiculous I became. At one point, I even convinced myself that maybe—just maybe—if I stared at the phone long enough, I could will a message into existence.
Spoiler: It didn't work.

Stage 3: Idealization.

Now this was the fun part. The part where everything about her seemed perfect. She was a goddess, and I was her humble admirer. Every little thing she did became an act of grace. I swear, she could sneeze and I would consider it the most majestic thing I'd ever witnessed.

"Wow, look at how gracefully she sneezed. I could learn a thing or two from her."

I started turning every interaction into something out of a fairy tale. When she smiled, it was like the sun came out from behind the clouds. When she laughed? Well, that was basically the soundtrack to my life. I had fallen into the trap of seeing her as this perfect, untouchable being.

And let's be real, I started imagining the life we could have together. It wasn't just about dates and romance—it was about the future. Yeah, I was already picking out wedding colors in my head. What? You don't do that? Well, I guess it's just me then.

Everything about her became a work of art. And of course, my brain started to idealize every moment we'd shared. I'd replay her saying my name in my head, as if it was the most sacred thing. "Did she say it with a hint of affection? Maybe?" I was practically creating a shrine to these perfect little moments in my mind, completely disregarding reality.

Stage 4: Frustration.

At some point, my idealized world collided with the reality of the situation. And let me tell you, it was a mess. Texts that should've been easy to send—like simple hellos—suddenly felt like they were life-or-death decisions. "Should I text her now?" "What if I text too much? What if I seem too eager? What if she never replies?" All these questions whizzing through my brain like a never-ending game of ping-pong.

I'd stare at the screen, then delete the message. And then, of course, I'd send it again. Rinse, repeat. This cycle of overthinking left me frustrated beyond belief. I felt like I was walking through mud, trying to figure out what to say without sounding completely insane.

But I did the only thing I knew best: I overcompensated. I tried to act casual, like nothing was wrong. "Hey, what's up?" I'd type. But inside, my heart was pounding like a jackhammer. My messages started to feel like a game of hide-and-seek. "Will she respond? Or am I just sending these messages into the void?"

Stage 5: Disappointment.

The next stage was inevitable. The disappointment hit like a cold splash of water on my face. It wasn't like she was being rude or dismissive; it was just that she didn't seem to feel the same way. And that was the harshest truth of all.

I had built up this grand vision of us together, and the reality was nothing like that. The messages I received, though polite, were short and distant. I'd keep reading them, hoping for some hidden meaning, some sign that she liked me back. But deep down, I knew it wasn't happening. The fantasy had crumbled, and what was left was just... silence.

It's like trying to make a sandcastle with wet sand. You think it's going to hold, but as soon as you try to shape it, it all falls apart.

Stage 6: Acceptance.

I hit a point where I realized, "This is it." I had to accept that I might never get the love I wanted. And you know what? It wasn't the end of the world. It wasn't like my life was suddenly over. I could still be happy. It was just that I had to stop clinging to an illusion.

Sure, it hurt like hell. But I started seeing the bigger picture. Maybe I didn't need her to love me back. Maybe I just needed to love myself enough to move on. Acceptance wasn't about giving up; it was about letting go of something I couldn't control. And that was a strange kind of freedom.

Stage 7: Hope.

And here I am now. Still hoping. Still waiting. But the hope isn't the same as before. It's not a desperate hope, but one that acknowledges that maybe, just maybe, something will change. Maybe I'll move on, or maybe—who knows?—she'll notice me in a way I never expected. Either way, I'll be okay.

I've realized that waiting doesn't have to be a sad thing. It's okay to hope. It's okay to still believe in something. And while I may not be at the end of this journey yet, I'm getting there. Slowly. Maybe I'm just a hopeless romantic who believes in love even when it seems impossible. But who knows? Sometimes the best stories have the most unexpected endings.
And who doesn't like a good underdog story?

So, yeah. Here I am, still waiting. Still hoping. And maybe, just maybe, this story isn't over yet.

This is the story of how one word ruined me (in the most ridiculous, heartwarming way possible).

Chanmi: One Word, Infinite Cling

Alright, let's be real here. This is the story of a guy (me, obviously) who tried his best to carve a tiny little corner in her heart. Spoiler alert: it didn't exactly go as planned. But hey, it's worth a laugh, so let's dive into the saga of the one and only Chanmi-the name that rocked my world for a grand total of one time

You see, I had this brilliant idea: "What if I convince her to give me a nickname? Something no one else calls me. Something... special." Genius, right? Wrong. Turns out, asking someone to give you a nickname is like asking them to remember your birthday-it's a lot of pressure for something they didn't sign up for.

But I was determined. I cornered her one day (figuratively, not literally-I'm not a creep), smiled my best "I'm harmless, I swear smile, and said, "Can you call me something? Just once? Something only you'll call me?"

She hesitated. I'm pretty sure she was weighing her options between calling me crazy and just walking away. But then, like a bolt of lightning from the heavens, she said it. Chanmi.

BOOM. Fireworks. Angels singing. My soul left my body for a second. It wasn't just a word; it was THE word. I looked at her with the kind of awe usually reserved for sunsets and free pizza. "Did she just say it?!" my brain screamed. Yes, she did, and for a moment, I was the happiest idiot on the planet.

But here's where the humor kicks in. She. Never. Said. It. Again. That's right-one and done Like a limited-edition product, Chanmi was a one-time offer. And me? Oh, I latched onto that single word like my life depended on it. I started calling myself Chanmi in my head, hoping one day she'd casually drop it again. Spoiler alert: she didn't.

And it's not like I didn't try. I'd subtly bring it up like, "Remember when you called me Chanmi? That was nice, right? You could, you know, do it again..." Her response? A smile. No word. Just a smile. And not the "aw, cute" kind. It was more like, "Why is this guy so obsessed with a nickname?"

Here's the painful part (because comedy without pain is just a stand-up routine): she never cared about it the way I did. For her, it was just a throwaway moment, a passing comment she probably forgot the second it left her lips. For me, though, it was everything.
But here's the kicker-Chanmi was never just a nickname. It was a word that, for some reason, only fit when it came from her lips. It wasn't just a name; it was a part of her. It sounded right when she said it, like it was a secret language between us, a little something only we shared. And, well... no one else can make it sound the way she did. It belonged to her, and now, it's stuck with me.

I know I'm being ridiculous. I'm the one who begged for it,

clung to it, turned it into a lifelong memory, and here I am, narrating it like some tragic love story. But you know what? That's the beauty of it. Love turns the tiniest things into treasures-and also turns you into a certified clown.

So here I am, the self-declared Chanmi ambassador, holding onto a nickname that doesn't even exist in her vocabulary anymore. She's out there living her life, probably laughing at memes and enjoying her world, while I'm sitting here wondering if I should add "Chanmi" to my passport.

But you know what? It's okay. I've realized something: she's not mine, never was, and probably never will be. She's someone else's chapter, while I'm here, still stuck in mine. And that one moment when she said Chanmi-that's my keepsake. My little memory of something sweet, something only hers, even if she never said it again.

So, yeah. It's bittersweet. I'm probably the only one who can say that I'm laughing at my own heartbreak. But that's the thing about love-it makes you hold monto things you shouldn't, makes you cling to moments that never really mattered to anyone but you.

And maybe, just maybe, somewhere down the line, she'll remember that word. Maybe not, though. But hey, I've got it. Chanmi. It's mine. It fits in my heart, and that's enough.

And if anyone asks, I'll just smile and say, "Yeah, she called me Chanmi... once.

Part III – The Storm

"Penguin"

Funny, isn't it? He calls you that—

The same word she teased me with, flat.

Once made me laugh, now makes me bleed,

A nickname now your heart might need.

I wonder, do you think of me,

When he says it so casually?

Or has my name, my care, my cries,

Vanished beneath his warmer skies?

CHAPTER THREE

The Question That Never Fades

Introduction: The Unspoken Question

Love has a way of carving itself into the deepest corners of our hearts — quietly, relentlessly, and sometimes without permission. It doesn't ask if we're ready; it simply arrives, planting itself like a seed and growing roots that intertwine with our very being. And once it's there, it becomes impossible to ignore. It lingers in the quiet spaces, in the unspoken words, in the longing glances that stretch just a little too long. Love makes a home inside us, even when it knows it may never be returned.

But what happens when that love remains hidden, unexpressed? When the heart you pour yourself into never quite reaches back to hold yours? When every moment shared feels like a gift and a curse — a reminder of how close you are to the person you cherish, and yet, how painfully distant you remain? It's a cruel paradox: feeling like someone is your entire world while realizing you might be nothing more than a fleeting moment in theirs.

There's a unique kind of ache in wondering where you stand in someone's life. It's the ache of waiting for a message that might never come, of hoping for a glance that might never turn your way. It's the ache of replaying conversations, dissecting every word, searching for hidden meaning — as if, buried beneath their kindness, there might be a trace of the love you so desperately crave. It's the ache of carrying a question that swells inside you like a storm, echoing in your chest over and over again:
Am I important to you?

This question becomes a shadow, haunting every interaction. It makes you second-guess your worth, your presence, your very existence in their life. Are you just another face in the crowd? Another name in a list of people who come and go? Or do you linger in their thoughts the way they linger in yours?

This is a story of that ache. Of loving in silence. Of holding on to fragments of hope, even as they slip through trembling fingers. It's a story of searching for significance in someone else's life while slowly losing pieces of yourself in the process. It's about the quiet pain of always being the one who cares more, who tries harder, who stays longer — even when the signs tell you to walk away.

But this story isn't just about heartbreak. It's about the bittersweet beauty of loving someone enough to step back, even when it breaks you. It's about the strength it takes to choose someone's happiness over your own. It's about learning that sometimes, love isn't about possession or reciprocation — sometimes, it's about letting go, even when your soul aches to hold on.

If you've ever loved someone from a distance, if you've ever stayed up at night wondering whether your absence would even be noticed, if you've ever whispered "Do I matter to you?" into the void of unanswered texts and empty silences — then this is for you.

This is the unfiltered truth of a heart that loved too deeply, too silently. A heart that shattered under the weight of its own longing, and yet, found the courage to love anyway. Because sometimes the truest form of love is the one that sacrifices itself for the sake of another's happiness.

And sometimes, the hardest goodbye is the one we never get to say out loud.

Part 1: "The Question of My Worth"

I sat in the quiet of my room, the hum of the world around me fading into a blur, while my mind kept returning to one question that gnawed at my soul—"Am I important to you?" It was as if the words floated in the air, taunting me, waiting for an answer I wasn't sure would ever come. It wasn't just any question—it was the one that held my heart captive, the one that made me look at every moment we had shared and wonder if it meant anything to you at all.

I had always admired you, seen you as a princess in your own world, someone who was unreachable yet captivating in every way. Your grace, your smile, the way you carried yourself—it all felt like something out of a fairy tale. And yet, here I was, in the real world, struggling with the weight of an emotion that seemed so one-sided. Was I important in your life? Did I matter to you in any way, or was I simply a passing moment, like a leaf carried by the wind, drifting in and out of your life without ever being noticed?

It wasn't that you had said anything that made me feel this way. It wasn't even that you had intentionally pushed me aside. It was the silence that spoke louder than any word could. The silence between us always seemed to scream the loudest, echoing with unspoken feelings. I would wait for you to reply to my messages, to initiate a conversation, and when it didn't come, I was left wondering—did I matter to you? Did I mean anything in your world?

You were a princess to me, someone so wrapped in the glow of her own life that I sometimes felt like an invisible shadow at the edges, watching but never truly seen. I couldn't help but ask myself if I had any place in your heart, any significance in your thoughts. Was I just a name you typed into your phone when you had a moment to spare, or was I someone who could occupy space in your heart, in your life?

It wasn't easy to admit, but I couldn't help but feel that I was always the one reaching out, always the one to show care, while you remained distant, lost in your own world. Sometimes, when I would try to get your attention, it felt like I was asking for too much. I would wonder, in those moments, if you even noticed me at all. If I walked past you, if I spoke to you, was there any part of you that recognized me for who I truly was, beyond the surface, beyond the mask I wore?

I wanted to believe that I mattered. I wanted to believe that you, with your laughter, your smile, and your warmth, saw me for what I was. But every time I was met with silence, that belief wavered. It was hard to keep holding on to the idea that I meant something when I couldn't feel it from you. And so, I kept asking myself the same question over and over: Am I important to you?

In the quiet of my room, I began to wonder if I was simply one of many names in your life, another face in the crowd. After all, you had so many people around you—friends, acquaintances, those who knew you better than I ever could. Did I even have a place among them? Or was I just a passing thought, something that didn't truly matter in the grand scheme of your life?

I had always felt as if I was on the outside, looking in. I would watch you from a distance, seeing the way you interacted with everyone, the way you laughed with your friends, shared your thoughts with them, and I couldn't help but feel left out. It wasn't jealousy. It was a sense of longing. A longing to be seen by you, to be understood, to be acknowledged for the person I truly was. But despite all the moments I shared with you, I still felt invisible. I could never fully express what was in my heart, afraid that if I did, it might push you even further away.

But there was something inside me, something deep, that told me to keep hoping, to keep trying. I couldn't shake the feeling that there was something between us, something unspoken that I was too afraid to confront. I wondered if you had ever felt the same, even in the quietest of moments. Had you ever stopped and thought about me? Did I ever cross your mind when you were busy, when you were lost in the whirlwind of your own life? Did I mean anything to you? Did I matter to you, at all?

I knew it wasn't fair to ask these things without ever voicing them. But the fear of rejection, the fear that I might be putting myself out there only to be met with indifference, held me back. I couldn't bear the thought of you looking at me and seeing nothing more than a fleeting moment. The idea of losing what little connection we had was too painful to even consider.

And so, I stayed silent, hoping for a sign, any sign, that would tell me where I stood in your life. Every glance, every smile, every word felt like a puzzle I couldn't quite solve. Were you truly just being kind, or was there something more behind it? Was I imagining things, or did you feel something for me that you couldn't quite put into words? The uncertainty gnawed at me, eating away at my peace.

In moments of quiet contemplation, I began to question my own worth. Was I enough? Was I worthy of being in your life? I wanted so much for you to see me—not just the facade I showed the world, but the real me beneath it all. The me that was vulnerable, the me that felt more than I could express, the me that longed to be valued. But the silence around me made it hard to know where I stood.

I couldn't help but wonder if I was asking for too much.

Was I wrong to want more? Was I wrong to want to know that I mattered to you, that I was not just a passing figure in your life but someone you held dear? In the quiet moments, I asked myself if I was being selfish, wanting your attention, wanting your care, wanting to know that I was important to you. But deep down, I knew it wasn't selfish. It was simply the truth of my heart. I needed to know. I needed to hear it from you, to have my fears silenced with the clarity of your words.

"Am I important to you?" I wondered, and though I was afraid to ask you aloud, I felt like the question was tattooed on my soul, running through my thoughts, piercing through the silence between us. But how could I ask you something so vulnerable, so open, without exposing everything I had hidden inside me? How could I ask you to answer a question that carried so much weight, so much longing, when I was afraid that your answer might be the one thing I couldn't bear to hear?

I had never told you this, but every time I saw you, a part of me hoped that maybe this time, you would look at me and see me for who I truly was. Not just a face in the crowd, not just another person who existed in your world, but someone who cared deeply, someone who needed to know that they mattered to you.

So here I am, with the question still burning in my heart—Am I important to you? Am I more than just another person in your life? Am I someone who has a place in your heart, even if it's just a small one? Or am I simply passing through, unnoticed, unimportant, drifting away like a forgotten whisper in the wind?

I don't know if you'll ever answer that question, and maybe that's okay. Maybe the answer lies within me, within my own sense of self-worth. But even so, I can't help but wonder, as I sit here in the silence of my thoughts—Am I important to you?

Part 2: "The Only One Who Matters"

As I sit here, struggling to find the right words to express what's inside me, it feels as though the weight of the entire world is pressing down on my chest. Every word I think of seems too small to capture the depth of my emotions, yet I know I must say it. For you. For me. For both of us, even though we may never truly see each other again in the same light.

This moment, this confession, is not something I ever imagined I would have to make. But here I am, at the crossroads of love, loss, and letting go. I never wanted it to come to this, but the truth is undeniable. I know now that the best thing I can do for you—perhaps the most selfless thing—is to step away from your life. This is not because I don't care, but because I care too much.

I've spent countless nights lying awake, thinking about the same question: Do I matter to you? And while the answer has never come directly from your lips, I've come to understand something profound and painful. The truth is, I may never matter the way I wish I did, the way my heart desperately hopes. I am not the one you need in your life, and deep down, I've always known it. You're the princess of your own world, and you deserve someone who will lift you up, not weigh you down.

There are times in life when you realize that love, as much as it burns, doesn't always lead to a happy ending. Sometimes love means letting go. Sometimes, it's about setting someone free to be who they are, without the emotional baggage of someone else's feelings tying them down. I don't want to be the complication in your life. I don't want to be the constant source of confusion and doubt. I don't want you to have to carry the burden of my unspoken love for you anymore. It's not fair to you, and it's certainly not fair to me.

You've been so strong, so independent, so perfect in your own way. And I've watched you from afar, silently admiring everything about you. Your grace, your beauty, your brilliance—it's all been so inspiring, so breathtaking. But through all of that, I've come to realize that I am not the person who can support you in the way that you deserve. I've been holding on to something that isn't mine to hold, and that's the painful truth I've come to face.

I never wanted to be a burden to you. But somehow, in my attempt to be close, to be present in your life, I've become one. My feelings, my attachment, my longing—all of it has become a weight you never asked for. You've never asked me to stay. You've never asked for anything from me, and yet I've continued to give, to hope, to dream. And now, as I sit here, looking back at everything we've shared—those fleeting moments, those quiet exchanges, those glances that meant everything to me—I understand that all of it was nothing more than a beautiful illusion.

I need to leave. Not because I want to, but because it's the only way for both of us to be free. For you to be free, and for me to finally let go of this painful attachment. You see, I've spent so much time holding onto this idea of us, this notion that maybe, just maybe, you would see me the way I see you. But I have to accept the reality that it's not meant to be. You don't need me. You never have.

I know that I've made things complicated. I know that my feelings have interfered with your life, even if you never noticed it. And the last thing I want is for you to feel trapped by my emotions. You deserve to be happy, to live your life without the pressure of my unrequited love hanging over you. You deserve to be surrounded by people who love you in the way you need, who can be there for you without hesitation or doubt. You deserve someone who can make you smile, who can bring joy into your life, without the sadness of unspoken words. And I am not that person.

I am stepping away because, for your sake, I must. I want you to live your life freely, without the weight of my feelings slowing you down. You deserve peace, happiness, and the opportunity to grow without the constant worry of how my heart feels. You deserve someone who can give you everything you need, without holding anything back. And as much as I want to be that person, I know that I can't.

There's something I need you to understand: this is not about me. This is not about my pain or my broken heart. This is about you. This is about letting you go, so that you can live the life you were always meant to live, without the shadows of my love haunting you. You are the only one who matters. Not me. I have come to realize that true love is not about holding on, but about knowing when to let go. And in this moment, with a heart that aches beyond words, I am letting you go.

It's hard to say goodbye, harder than I ever imagined. But I know it's the right thing to do. I know that in order for you to truly live, I must step aside. And as much as it hurts, I believe this is the best thing for both of us. You don't need me. You never did. I was just someone who, for a while, took up space in your life. But now, I must leave, so that you can be free of me, so that you can be free of this invisible burden I've placed on you.

I can't keep clinging to something that isn't mine. I can't keep hoping that you will one day see me the way I see you, because I know in my heart that it's not going to happen. And as much as I wish I could be the one to make you happy, I know that I can't. I'm not the person you need. And so, I must let go.

You are the only one who matters. And in this moment, I am putting you first. I am doing what's best for you, even if it means breaking my own heart. I am leaving because it's the only way for you to find peace. I am leaving because, in my heart, I know that this is the best thing I can do for you. You deserve everything good in this world, and I can't keep standing in the way of that.

I will carry my love for you in silence, in the quiet corners of my heart, where it will never be seen. You will never know the depth of my feelings, the strength of my emotions, because it's not for you to know. It's not for you to carry. And so, I will carry it alone, silently, forever. You will be the princess of your own world, and I will step back, knowing that I did the right thing, even if it broke me to do it.

Goodbye, my princess. I hope you find the happiness you deserve. I hope you find someone who can be there for you in the way that I always wished I could be. You will always be in my heart, even if I can never be in yours. And in the quiet moments, when I think of you, I will remember you not as the person who broke my heart, but as the person who taught me the true meaning of love—love that lets go, love that sacrifices for the sake of the other person's happiness.

And with that, I say goodbye.
When love orbits just out of reach, the soul sings quietly to the night:

A MOON NOT MINE ~♡~

My moon belongs to another star, Yet I adore her from afar. Her light so gentle, calm, and bright, Guides my dreams through the silent night.

You asked me, Sinamoti, why she? Here is the reason, plain to see.

She's the poem my heart chose to write, The melody that lingers through the night

Her smile holds worlds my soul longs to see, That's why, Sinamoti, it's she for me. Her presence feels like a gentle breeze, Calming storms, putting my mind at ease.

She orbits close, yet far away, A distant glow I can't betray. She doesn't even know, yet she's the key To dreams that whisper, "It must be she."

Though she's not mine, my heart does yearn, To feel her warmth, to have her turn. But stars decide their destined course, And love, at times, must stay remorse.

So I'll keep watching, heart confined, A moon not mine, yet still divine. For in her glow, my soul finds peace, Even if longing may never cease.

Part IV – The Abyss

"If Only I Mattered"

I speak in silence, you never hear,
I stand beside, yet disappear.
I give, I give, until I'm dust,
Still praying that you see me just—

As someone more than passing air,
As someone here, who's always there.
But maybe I was made to fade,
In love's grand stage, behind the shade

CHAPTER FOUR

The Love That Stays, Even When You Don't

Introduction

Love is often painted as a beautiful, uplifting force — the spark that brings color to our world. But love, in its truest form, is not always easy or painless. It's a spectrum of emotions, a storm of feelings that can lift you to the highest peaks and drag you to the deepest depths. And sometimes, the most profound act of love is not holding on but learning to let go.

This chapter is a journey through the quiet ache of unspoken words, the sting of jealousy, and the bittersweet realization that loving someone means wanting their happiness above all else — even if it means stepping back. It's a reflection on the beauty and pain of first love, the lessons it teaches, and the strength it takes to set someone free while carrying their memory as a quiet ember in your heart.

Here, love is not about possession but about respect, not about demanding a place in someone's life but about honoring their choices. And even in the letting go, love remains — steadfast, patient, and unwavering. Because sometimes, love is not about finding a way to stay but about finding peace in the distance.

Let this chapter be a testament to the power of love's quiet sacrifice — a heart that breaks but beats on, carrying love not as a burden, but as a gift.

Part : 1

There are moments in life that change us—moments that shape us, teach us, and force us to see ourselves in a different light. You, in your own quiet, effortless way, gave me more than just memories. You gave me an entire spectrum of emotions—emotions I never even knew I was capable of feeling. You allowed me to experience the highest highs and the deepest lows.

I've come to realize that love is not just about the good times, the laughter, or the sweet moments shared. It's also about the painful, bittersweet ones—the times when you sit in silence, contemplating feelings that run too deep for words. And you, in all your grace, made me feel all of it. The joy, the pain, the longing, the confusion—it was a whirlwind, and I was caught in it.

But you also gave me something I never expected: jealousy. At first, I couldn't understand it. Why did it hurt so much when I saw you with someone else? I never thought of myself as the jealous type, but there I was, struggling with something that seemed so foreign to me. Watching you laugh with another, seeing someone else hold your attention the way I wished I could, it stung more than I cared to admit.

But you know what? In the end, I had to accept it. Because if there's one thing I've learned, it's that jealousy comes from caring deeply. And I cared for you more than I ever thought possible. It wasn't about possession or control. It was about wanting to protect something so precious, something that meant so much to me. But the reality is, I don't own you. I never did.

You are your own person, and you have every right to choose who you want in your life. And no matter what, I will always respect your choice. Always. You're free to do what makes you happy, free to choose anyone who makes you feel valued and loved the way you deserve. Because in the end, your happiness is all that matters to me.

It took me a while to understand that. To realize that love doesn't come with chains or restrictions. It's not about ownership—it's about wanting the best for someone, even if that means letting them go. And that's exactly what I've learned. I want you to live your life, to be free to chase your dreams and desires, without any hesitation, without any constraints.

I still remember one thing you told me so clearly. It's

something that's stayed with me all this time. I asked you once, in a moment of vulnerability, what you truly desired, what you wanted out of life. You looked at me, with that quiet strength you always carried, and said, "I want to live, not just survive."

Those words hit me harder than I expected. They made me realize that we don't live just to exist, to go through the motions. We live to feel, to experience, to grow. To be free. To truly live.

But as for me, my desire? It's simpler, really. More than anything, I want to be the one who helps make your dreams come true. I want to be the one who stands by your side, supporting you in every way I can. Even if I can't be the one to hold your hand in the end, I want to make sure you have someone who can—someone who will care for you as deeply as I do.

You are my first love, and I can't quite find the words to express what that means to me. Loving you, even from a distance, has been both the most beautiful and the most painful experience of my life. You've taught me what it means to love selflessly, to put someone else's happiness before my own, and to respect their choices—no matter how much it hurts.

I can't express the depth of what you mean to me in a few simple lines. It's something that lives in the quiet spaces between words, something that lingers in the heart long after the conversations end.

But I want you to know this: you are unforgettable. Even if

our paths never cross the way I imagined, you will always be the one who taught me the true meaning of love. You will always be the first to leave an imprint on my soul.

And now, as I look at the world around me, I realize that love is not about expecting anything in return. It's about giving without expecting. It's about wanting someone's happiness more than your own. And even if that means letting go, I'm okay with it. Because your happiness is what matters most.

I'm still here, still grateful for everything you've taught me, still hoping, still learning, and still respecting every choice you make.

You'll always have a place in my heart, and I'll always wish you the best.
But as much as I say that, as much as I tell myself I can let go, there's always that tiny part of me that can't quite do it. The part of me that still hopes, that still holds on to the smallest thread of possibility. Maybe it's foolish, maybe it's unrealistic, but it's the truth. And I don't mind admitting that.

I suppose it's the nature of love, isn't it? To cling to something, even when you know it might not be for you. Even when you know the chances of it ever becoming real are as slim as the faintest star in the night sky. But that doesn't stop the heart from yearning. And maybe, just maybe, I'll always have that quiet hope tucked away somewhere inside me.

I'll wait—if not forever, then until the day I finally learn how to move on. Until I find the strength to face the truth head-on and walk away, knowing that you have found what makes you happy. But until then, I'm here. Still here, hoping that life will lead you toward everything you deserve, even if I can't be the one to walk by your side.

And even if you never realize it, even if you never know how deeply I feel, I will still respect your choices. You are the one who deserves to choose. Whether it's the love of your life, your career, or your dreams—I will never stand in the way of that.

You see, I've realized something even deeper about love. It's not just about holding on; it's also about the freedom to let go. I'm learning to give you that freedom, because love that binds you too tightly isn't love at all. It's more like a cage. And you deserve to soar free, to make your own decisions, to carve your own path. You've taught me that. And for that, I'm forever grateful.

It's also funny how, despite the pain, I look back and smile at the memory of your words, "I want to live, not just survive." I find myself repeating them, almost like a mantra, whenever I feel like I'm losing my way. It's a reminder that life is more than just existing—it's about thriving, about feeling alive. And I'll do that, too, one day. I'll learn to live without this weight on my heart.

But until then, I'll carry this experience with me. I'll cherish it, even if it's painful. I'll cherish it because you were the first to show me what true love is. And you are still, and will always be, my first love—the one who changed everything for me.

Now, as I stand here, waiting for whatever comes next, I feel a strange sense of peace. I'm not angry. I'm not bitter. I don't feel resentful or hurt in the way I once did. Instead, I feel gratitude. Gratitude for everything you've given me, for every word you've spoken, for every smile you've shared with me. Even if it was never meant for me in the way I wanted, it was still a gift.

You see, I've learned that love isn't just about getting what you want. It's about giving. Giving without expecting. I'll never stop caring for you. Even if it's from a distance, I'll always hope for your happiness.

You're free to choose who you want, free to follow your dreams. And no matter who you choose, I'll respect that decision. Because your happiness is more important than anything else. I might never be the one to walk beside you, but that doesn't change the way I feel about you.

And as I finally come to accept this, there's one thing I know for sure: You were never just a passing moment for me. You were never just a fleeting thought. You were my first love, and I'll carry that with me always. Even if we never meet again in the way I imagined, your memory will stay with me forever.

You taught me that love isn't about ownership or possession. It's about respect. It's about learning to let go when you have to, and finding peace with it. And I've found my peace, knowing that you will always have a place in my heart.

Thank you, for showing me what it means to love, what it means to care, and what it means to let go. Thank you, for teaching me the deepest lesson I could have learned: that love is freedom. And in your freedom, I will always find my peace.

The Devotion

"Her Smile, My Religion"

I never prayed until I saw,
The way you smiled—without a flaw.
And ever since, my faith was you,
In every tear, in every blue.

I gave you all, yet asked for none,
Not even a moon beneath your sun.
Love isn't holding—it's letting be.
Even if it breaks what's left of me.

CHAPTER FIVE

The Weight of Unspoken Love

Introduction

What happens when love becomes too heavy to carry in silence? When the heart, no longer able to bear the burden of unspoken words, breaks open and spills every hidden feeling onto the page? This chapter delves into the painful beauty of loving someone from afar — the longing, the sacrifice, and the quiet devastation of knowing your heart beats for someone who may never return your love.

After years of holding back, he finally confesses through a letter — a fragile piece of his soul wrapped in words and a single rose. But instead of relief, his confession brings a storm of heartbreak. She reads his letter, acknowledges his love, and promises friendship. Yet, as he clings to that promise, she disappears without explanation, leaving him drowning in unanswered questions.

Just when he begins to accept the unbearable truth of her absence, a late-night message reignites the agony. She read the letter again. But why? Curiosity? Regret? Or is there something she can't bring herself to say? The uncertainty gnaws at him, dragging him through sleepless nights and endless wandering, searching for pieces of her in places they once dreamed of visiting together.

But fate isn't done with him yet. One night, beneath the dim glow of a streetlight, he sees her again — holding the letter, her face shadowed with sadness. And in that moment, everything changes.

This chapter is a haunting exploration of love that lingers like a ghost, of hope that refuses to die, and of the heartbreaking realization that sometimes loving someone means loving them... even when they can't love you back the same way.

Part : 1

Love, I learned, isn't always loud. Sometimes, it's a quiet ache that lingers beneath your skin, a longing that never fades, no matter how many times you tell yourself to move on. For years, I carried that ache like a second heartbeat — a constant reminder that my heart belonged to someone who never asked for it. Someone who never even knew just how deeply I loved her.
She wasn't just a girl to me. She was everything.
My princess.
My ma'am..
And, most painfully, a penguin — a nickname I once cherished, now shared with someone else who had the privilege of standing closer to her than I ever could.

I loved her the way poets write tragedies — with an intensity that consumed me, even when I tried to bury it. I loved her in silence, convincing myself that friendship was enough, that as long as I could see her smile and hear her laugh, I didn't need anything more. I told myself that love didn't need to be spoken to be real. That I could hold onto my feelings like a secret, and maybe, just maybe, that would be enough to keep her close.

But love doesn't stay hidden forever. It grows, swells, and eventually, it spills over — no matter how tightly you try to contain it.
I wrote her a letter.

I don't know what I hoped would happen when I put pen to paper. Maybe it was a desperate attempt to release the weight I'd carried for so long. Or maybe, deep down, I wanted her to know — even if it changed nothing. I wanted her to understand that she had been the light in my darkness, the reason I kept going when everything else felt meaningless.
The letter wasn't just words; it was a piece of my soul.

I filled it with our conversations, the little moments I had replayed in my mind a thousand times. The times she called me by my nickname, chanmi, even if only once. That single word had become my lifeline, a reminder that, for at least a fleeting moment, I mattered to her. I wrote about how she taught me love's beauty, but also its agony. How I learned to be selfless because loving her meant putting her happiness above my own.

I placed a rose inside the letter — a symbol of love and pain,

delicate petals hiding sharp thorns. And I added a poem, my words bleeding onto the page like an open wound.
But I couldn't give it to her myself.

I was a coward when it came to her. Afraid that speaking my truth would shatter the fragile bond we shared. So I handed the letter to Monjulika, hoping she would keep my secret a little longer. But fate, it seems, had other plans. The letter found its way to her hands. And then, after days of agonizing silence, my phone buzzed with a message.
Her name lit up my screen, and my heart stopped.

"Hey... well, got your letter today. Wanted to talk nicely about it, but I will talk to you after your examinations... since don't want to disturb. And yea... I am sorry I couldn't wish you luck earlier because of my mother... so yea, best of luck for the remaining exams. I would definitely say you will never lose me as a friend...."

I read the message over and over again, each word slicing through me like a blade.
"You will never lose me as a friend."
Friend.

The word felt like a death sentence. After everything I'd poured into that letter, after finally confessing the feelings I had buried for three long years, all she could offer me was friendship. A place in her life, yes — but never the place I truly wanted.

I tried to tell myself I should be grateful. That her kindness was a gift, even if it wasn't love. But my heart rebelled against the logic. I wanted more. I wanted her.

In a haze of heartbreak, I typed back the words that had
been clawing at my chest for years:
"I'll wait for you till my last breath, and that's my promise."

It wasn't a plea or an attempt to change her mind. It was
just the truth. I had loved her for so long that the idea of
stopping felt impossible. I didn't know how to exist without
loving her.

But then... she blocked me.
Without warning. Without explanation.
Just gone.

I stared at my phone, disbelief crashing over me like a tidal
wave. My heart pounded, my hands shook, and my vision
blurred with tears I couldn't hold back. The world around
me disappeared, shrinking to the cold glow of my screen
and the emptiness she left behind.

I wanted to scream. To beg the universe to rewind time,
to undo whatever I had done to make her cut me off so
suddenly. I replayed every conversation, every interaction,
trying to figure out where I went wrong. Had my love been
too much? Had I overwhelmed her? Or was she simply
relieved to finally sever the tie that bound us?

I'll never know.
All I know is that one moment, she was there — and the
next, she wasn't.

I sank into my bed, clutching my phone to my chest like
it could somehow bring her back. My mind spiraled with

questions, but none of them had answers. I felt hollow, as if she had taken a piece of me when she left, a piece I could never get back.

"You will never lose me as a friend."

The words echoed through my skull like a cruel joke. But the truth was, I had lost her — not just as a friend, but as the person who had unknowingly kept me afloat when I was drowning.

And now, all I had left were memories.

Memories of stolen moments and words left unsaid. Memories of a love so fierce it burned me from the inside out.

Memories of a girl who once called me chanmi — and then walked away.

I loved her.

I still love her.

And maybe I always will.

Part 2 : The Ghost of a Goodbye
(An Imaginary Continuation)

Days blurred into nights, and nights stretched into eternity. The world outside kept moving, but I stayed frozen in that last moment — the moment she disappeared from my life. I kept checking my phone like a fool, hoping for a miracle. Hoping her name would light up my screen, that she'd unblock me, that she'd say something, anything.

But silence was my only answer.

I stopped sleeping. My room became a tomb, and I was its ghost, haunting the memories of a love that never fully lived. The rose I had given her in the letter haunted me too — a cruel metaphor. Love and pain, wrapped in fragile petals and sharp thorns. I wondered if she had kept it or if she had thrown it away, just like she had thrown me out of her life.

I told myself I needed closure, but what I really wanted was hope.
And then, one night, it happened.
My phone buzzed at 3:17 AM.
It wasn't her. But it was close enough to break me all over again.
Monjulika.
I hesitated, my heart thudding painfully. My hands were trembling as I opened the message.
"She read your letter again today."
That was it.

Nothing more. No explanation. No promise that she'd come back. Just the simple fact that she had revisited my words. I stared at the message, my mind spiraling with possibilities. Why would she read it again? Was it curiosity? Guilt? Or some part of her that missed me too?

I typed and deleted a dozen responses. In the end, I settled on just one word:
"Why?"
Monjulika's reply came hours later, when the sun had already risen and my eyes were swollen from crying.

"I don't know. She didn't say anything. She just held the letter for a long time and looked sad. And then she left."

Sad.

That word lodged itself in my chest like a knife. I imagined her sitting alone, the letter in her hands, rereading all the words I had poured out for her. Maybe she hated me for confessing. Maybe she pitied me. Or maybe — and this was the thought that destroyed me — maybe she missed me too, but couldn't face what that meant.

I didn't text Monjulika back. What was the point? She didn't have the answers I needed. The only person who did had locked herself away from me.
And so, life dragged on.

I started walking aimlessly through the city at night, just to escape the four walls of my room. I'd wander for hours, my feet carrying me to places we had once talked about visiting together. A park she loved. A café she had mentioned in passing. A bookstore I thought she'd like. I walked, hoping the ache in my chest would eventually fade.
It never did.
But then, one night, I saw her.

I almost thought I was hallucinating. I blinked, rubbed my eyes, and yet — she was still there. Sitting alone on a bench in the park, her face illuminated by the dim glow of a streetlight. She was holding something in her lap, and my heart stopped when I realized what it was.
The letter.
My letter.

I stood frozen, torn between running to her and staying hidden in the shadows. Every rational part of me screamed to walk away, to let her be, to respect the distance she had put between us. But my heart — that foolish, relentless heart — didn't care about logic.

Before I knew what I was doing, I was walking toward her.

I didn't say her name. I didn't even breathe too loudly, afraid she'd vanish like a mirage. But she must have sensed me, because she looked up. And when her eyes met mine, something shattered between us — something fragile and unspoken, finally breaking open after all this time.

She didn't look angry. Or annoyed.
She looked tired. And sad.
And maybe a little bit relieved.
"Why?" I whispered, my voice barely audible.

Her fingers tightened around the letter. She looked down at it, her eyes glassy, like she was holding back tears. For a long time, she didn't speak, and I thought maybe she wouldn't. Maybe she'd just get up and leave again.

But then, she broke the silence.

"Because I don't know how to lose you without it hurting," she said softly.

Her words knocked the air out of my lungs. I opened my mouth, but no sound came out. She shook her head, tears slipping down her cheeks.

"I blocked you because I didn't know what else to do," she whispered. "I thought it would be easier. For you. For me. But it wasn't."

I dropped to my knees in front of her, the weight of everything crushing me. "Then why?" I choked out. "Why not just talk to me?"

She looked at me like I was a question she couldn't answer.

"Because you love me," she said, her voice breaking. "And I... I don't know if I can love you back the same way. And I didn't want to break you more than I already have."

I should have felt devastated. I should have fallen apart right then and there. But instead, I reached out and gently took her hand.

"You being here," I whispered, "is enough."
She cried. I cried.

We sat there, tangled in the mess of our feelings, in the wreckage of unspoken words and complicated love. And for the first time, I realized that maybe love isn't always about getting what you want. Maybe sometimes love is just about showing up, even when everything feels impossible.

We didn't fix everything that night. She didn't magically love me the way I loved her. But she let me stay. She let me be there. And in that moment, that was enough to keep my heart beating.
Maybe it always would be.

Author's Note:
This chapter is purely imaginary — a continuation my heart wishes for but reality may never grant. Perhaps in some alternate universe, she reads the letter and finds her way back to me. Perhaps in another life, I get to love her freely. But for now, this chapter exists only in the pages of my longing. And maybe, just maybe, that's enough.

In the silence of rejection, these words remained:

AM I NOTHING TO YOU?
I chose you, unknowingly you knew, You were my sun,
my sky, my view.
But your words fell sharp, they tore me apart, "I'm not
yours," echoed deep in my heart.
My efforts, my love-did they all go in vain?
Each step I took only deepened the pain.

To you, I'm nothing, just a passing phase, A shadow
unseen in the world's endless maze.
Do I matter? The thought drowns me whole, A question
unanswered that weighs on my soul.
Not to you, not to them, not to anyone near, Yet I keep
hoping, through every tear.
I gave you my all, but it wasn't enough, Your silence
screamed loud; your words were tough.

Still, I'm here, though you turn away, Loving you quietly,
day by day.
Am I someone in the story of your life? Or just a fleeting
page in your endless strife? Even if I don't, I'll love you
still, For unrequited love bends, but it won't kill.
"Am I supposed to mean something in your life, Or do my
efforts fade like whispers in strife? Do you see the care I
silently pour, Or am I just another face you ignore?"

The Goodbye Within

"Still Mine in My Heart"

They ask if I moved on from you,
I nod, like liars often do.
But every step away I take,
Still leads me back to hearts that ache.

You're not in arms, but still in breath,
In every thought that flirts with death.
They'll never know what I conceal—
A love unclaimed, yet just as real.

CHAPTER SIX

THE DAY I BECAME A GHOST

Introduction:

The last day of school wasn't supposed to feel this heavy.

I told myself I'd walk out of those gates with my head high, that leaving behind the walls where I first fell in love — and fell apart — would bring me peace. I convinced myself that letting go of the place where my heart learned both love and loss would be the first step to healing.

But as I stepped through the familiar hallways, every step dragged me deeper into memories I couldn't escape. The echoes of old laughter clung to the walls like shadows, and every corner held a reminder of her. The way she used to twirl her pen absentmindedly during class. The sound of her voice, teasing and soft, like a song only I could hear.

I thought I could fade away quietly. Slip out of her world without a trace, just another forgotten name on a class roster. That maybe, if I disappeared, the ache in my chest would disappear too.

But fate had other plans.
Because she was still there.
And the universe wasn't done breaking me yet.
I didn't want to see her. But I knew I would.
And the cruelest part?
I wasn't sure if she'd even notice I was gone.

Let's begin this chapter :

The last day felt heavier than I expected.

I walked through the school gates one final time, my bag slung carelessly over my shoulder, each step echoing with memories I wasn't ready to let go of. The corridors smelled the same — that strange blend of old books, chalk dust, and teenage dreams. But everything else felt different.

Because she was still here.

And I was leaving.

I passed by the classroom we used to share, my fingers brushing against the cold metal of the doorframe. I didn't dare peek inside. I didn't want to see her sitting there, her head tilted as she scribbled in her notebook, or worse — laughing at someone else's joke. I told myself it didn't matter anymore. That I was doing the right thing by leaving.

But my heart screamed otherwise.

I wondered if she noticed my absence. If she turned around in her seat and glanced toward the door, half-expecting me to walk in. Or if my presence had already faded, like writing on a fogged-up window — there for a moment, and then gone without a trace.

Monjulika tried to convince me to stay.

"She misses you," she said one afternoon, her voice quiet but firm. "She doesn't say it, but I can tell."

I had only smiled, the kind of smile that hurts more than a frown. "Missing someone isn't the same as wanting them to stay," I replied. "And she made her choice."

Monjulika didn't argue after that. Maybe she understood. Or maybe she just grew tired of watching me break myself apart for someone who didn't know how to catch the falling pieces.

The bell rang, jolting me back to reality. I kept walking, my steps slower, as if some foolish part of me believed that dragging my feet might stop time itself.

And then, as if the universe couldn't resist one last cruel twist — I saw her.

She was standing by the staircase, her hair catching the light in a way that made my chest ache. She was talking to her friends, smiling, looking so painfully alive while I felt like a ghost. I slipped behind a pillar, my body pressed against the cold wall, my heart hammering against my ribs.

I shouldn't have cared.

But I did.

I stayed there for longer than I should have, watching her from a distance like some tragic character in a novel. She laughed at something, her eyes crinkling at the corners, and I swear I felt my soul shatter. Because that laugh — the same laugh that used to feel like home — wasn't mine anymore.

Maybe it never was.

I clenched my jaw and turned away, forcing my feet to move. Every step I took away from her felt like tearing myself apart, thread by thread. But I didn't stop. I couldn't.

I reached the school gate, pausing for just a moment to glance back.
She didn't notice me.
She never even looked.
I walked out and didn't look back again.

Later that night, I wrote in my journal:

"Today, I left the school. I left the place where I fell in love, where I learned the taste of heartbreak, where I buried a version of myself that I can never resurrect. I don't know if she'll remember me a year from now. Or five. Or ever. But I know I'll remember her for the rest of my life. She'll be a scar I carry, a love story without an ending. And maybe that's okay. Maybe some people are meant to be chapters, not whole books."

I closed the journal, turned off the light, and lay in the darkness — hoping that maybe, in some parallel universe, she was missing me too.

Part 2 : The Boy Who Waited
(The Final Chapter)

Years slipped by like pages turning in the wind. Seasons changed, people came and went, but some things — some feelings — refused to fade.

I carried her with me everywhere, like a shadow I couldn't outrun.

I graduated. Moved to a different city. Built a life that looked normal from the outside. I learned how to laugh with friends, how to carry conversations without my voice shaking, how to sleep without crying into my pillow. I became an expert at pretending I was okay.

But at night, when the world quieted and the noise faded, she returned.

In the shape of a memory.
In the echo of a nickname that no one else would ever call me.
In the ghost of a love I never stopped feeling.

I wondered if she still had the letter. If the petals of that rose had withered, or if she had tossed it away the moment she blocked me. I never dared to ask Monjulika again — I didn't want to know. Not knowing kept hope alive, even if it was a fragile, foolish kind of hope.

And despite everything... I kept waiting.

I told myself I'd move on. That I'd meet someone new. That one day, I'd love someone who actually wanted to stay. But every time I tried, my heart dragged me back to her.

The truth was simple: I never wanted anyone else.

It didn't matter if she forgot me. It didn't matter if she was happy with someone else. I had promised her — promised myself — that I would wait for her until my last breath. And so, I did.

I waited.

Through birthdays she no longer remembered.
Through nights when my chest ached so badly, I thought my heart might give out.
Through the endless silence that stretched between us, growing heavier with each passing day.

I waited.

Not because I believed she would come back.
Not because I thought she still loved me, or even thought about me.
I waited... because loving her was the only thing I knew how to do.

And maybe that's what real love is — loving someone even when they don't love you back. Wanting their happiness, even when it destroys you. Holding onto the smallest spark of hope, even when the darkness tells you to let go.

I wrote a final entry in my journal on the anniversary of the day we first talked:

"It's been years, and I'm still waiting.

I don't know if you'll ever come back. Maybe you won't. Maybe you've built a life where I no longer exist, and that's okay. I just hope you're happy. I hope you've found someone who makes you laugh the way I always wished I could.

But if you ever get lost, if the world ever feels too heavy — just know that I'm still here.
Still waiting.
Still yours."

I closed the journal, placed it on my shelf, and turned off the light.
The night swallowed me whole, but I didn't fight it.
I just lay there, staring at the ceiling, my heart beating to the rhythm of her name.
And I waited.
I waited like I always did.
Like I always would.

When love faded, only this poem remained:

Silent Surrender

In every glance, I lose my way,
A prisoner of words I couldn't say.

I watched you pass, but stood afar,
Majboor hoon, beneath this silent star.

Your smile, a dagger, yet I spoke,
My fragile heart, with every word, broke.

I bared my soul, my love laid bare,
Hoping you'd see how much I care.

But you turned away, your heart not mine,
A love I treasured, lost in time.

I lost you, though I held on tight,
Majboor hoon, beneath love's fading light.

Now memories linger, sharp and cold,
A silent heart, with dreams untold.

Final Letter to Her

What You'll Never Read

Hey princess ,
I loved you more than I should've dared,
In moments you laughed, in days you cared.
But I chose silence—not because I'm weak,
But because your joy is all I seek.

If someday life feels heavy and wild,
Remember—once, you were someone's smile.
Not mine to hold, but mine to feel,
Forever love, forever real.

CHAPTER SEVEN

TALES IN VERSES

Starting : In these verses, I lay bare the thoughts that linger in the quiet spaces of my heart. They are my silent confessions.

1. The Weight of Waiting

I built a home in the silence you left behind,
Decorated it with memories I never lived,
Hung hope like fairy lights across the walls,
And called it love.

I slept in the corners where your voice once lingered,
Fed my soul with the echoes of old conversations,
Watered the flowers of my longing
With the tears I swore I wouldn't cry.

And every morning,
I opened the door —
Just in case you decided
To come back home.

2. Love That Lingers

Some people leave, but their shadow stays.
I've been dancing with yours for years,
My heart beating to the echo of your name,
My soul tracing the outline of a ghost.

I keep you in the corners of my mind,
A soft ache I don't want to heal.
Because forgetting you
Feels like losing you all over again.

So I carry you —
Not as a burden, but as a reminder
That love doesn't always end
When people do.

3. The Ache of Being Forgotten

I wonder if you remember me
The way I remember you —
Not as a person, but as a feeling
I can never name.

I wonder if your heart ever trips
Over the thought of me,
If my absence ever brushes against your skin
Like a cold breeze you can't explain.

Or maybe I'm just a faded photograph
Tucked away in the drawer of your past —
Forgotten.
But still there.

4. On Heartbreak

I didn't lose you all at once.
I lost you in fragments —
Each day stealing a little more of you
Until I was left with only absence.

I lost you in the way your texts got shorter,
In the spaces between your words,
In the way you laughed at my jokes
Like you were already halfway gone.

And by the time I realized
I was holding a love
You no longer wanted,
I had already bled myself dry
Trying to keep you.

5. The Tragedy of Unspoken Love

I loved you in every way except out loud.
Maybe that's why you never heard me.
I stitched your name into my chest,
Wrote you into every poem I never shared.

I watched you fall in love with others,
My heart breaking quietly,
Like glass cracking under the weight of longing
Too heavy to carry,
Too sacred to release.

And when you left,
I didn't chase after you —
Because I loved you too much
To make you stay.

6. For the longing that never fades:

I loved her in the quietest ways —
In the pauses between words,
In the spaces she never looked.
I loved her like a prayer unanswered,

A wish the universe refused to grant.
I memorized the shape of her smile,
Traced the outline of her laugh in my mind.
Every glance, a galaxy I lost myself in,
Every silence, a storm I couldn't outrun.

She walked through my life like a fleeting season,
But I stayed rooted, waiting for her return.
My heart, a garden that only knew her name,
Blooming with petals she never cared to pick.

7. For the heartbreak that lingers like a shadow:

She left,
But her absence stayed —
An unwelcome guest
That made a home in my chest.
Her name became a wound
I pressed on, over and over,
Just to feel something close to her touch.

I told myself I was healing,
But I was only learning to live with the pain.
I built monuments out of memories,
Lit candles for the love that died in my arms.
And when the nights grew too heavy to bear,
I whispered her name into the darkness,
Hoping the echo might bring her back.

8. For the relentless obsession:

I counted the days by her silence,
Named every hour after her.
My heart became a mausoleum
Of moments we never shared.

I chased her ghost through empty streets,
Found fragments of her in strangers' eyes.
The world became a cruel reminder
That she had touched my soul and let go.

I screamed into pillows just to muffle the ache,
Wrote her letters I'd never send.
Because even in my madness,
Loving her felt like the only truth I knew.

9. For the hope that refuses to die:

If she called my name,
Even in a whisper,
I'd run to her barefoot —
Even if the road was lined with thorns.

I'd unravel myself at her feet,
A tattered offering of love.
I'd carve a home for her in my ribs,
Let her rest there, forever untouched by pain.

She doesn't have to love me back.
She doesn't have to stay.
I'll love her enough for both of us —
A wildfire that never learns to die.

10. For the sacrifice that love demands:

If loving her meant burning,
Then let me be ash.
If forgetting her meant freedom,
Then let me stay chained to the past.

I would shatter for her a thousand times,
If it meant she could feel whole.
I would stitch my heart back together
With threads of her memory,
Only to watch it break again.

Because love, I've learned,
Isn't about holding on.
It's about loving someone enough
To let them go —
Even if it destroys you.

11. Fading Echoes of Lost Love

In the depths of despair, I find myself lost,
Devastated, defeated, at such a high cost.
I'm done with this longing, this painful wait,
Dying inside, for your love, my heart's heavy weight.

I hoped for your appearance, for your love so true,
But my expectations shattered, leaving me blue.
I thought you'd come, and say you love me so,
But now I know, that hope's long ago.

You won't approach, you won't be here,
My heart aches, with each passing tear.
I thought you'd show, your love so grand,
But now I see, it's slipped from my hand.

I'm done with this pain, with this endless wait,
It hurts too much, it's sealing my fate.
You're done with me, I can clearly see,
But know this, your love will always be.

12. The Unspoken

Between the lines of every rhyme,
There lies a truth, unsold by time,
An unspoken love, a silent plea,
A heart that longe, but never free

Each word I write, each line I weave,
A testament to love's reprieve,
In every poem, a hidden part,
Of an unspoken, yearning heart.

13. Drifting Away

In a quiet realm,
I wander slow,
To a place where you might not go.

A world unknown,
yet I must leave,
Will you remember,
Will you grieve?

I don't know what I meant to you,
But you, my angel, pure and true.
Hold me close within your heart,
As I from this world depart.

If I reach that distant shore,
Will you keep my memory more?
Not as love, nor romance bright,
But as a star in your night.

Let me live in thoughts so kind,
In the corners of your mind.
Keep me alive, though I may roam,
In your heart, my lasting home.

14. The Grave of My Love

I buried your name beneath my tongue,
Hoping my words might taste less bitter.
But every sentence I speak
Is a funeral procession of memories.

I wear your absence like a shroud,
A ghost wrapped in my own skin.
And each time I try to resurrect myself,
I die in the shadow of your smile.

15. The Letter That Burned Me Instead

I wrote you a letter, but never sent it.
My hands shook, afraid of your silence.
I sealed the envelope with my tears,
And pressed my lips to your name like a final prayer.

I placed it in a drawer — a coffin for my words.
But the ink bled through the paper,
Staining my fingers, my soul, my existence.
I tried to write you out of my heart,
But love is not a poem that can be erased.

16. The Echo of Your Silence

Your silence speaks louder than your words ever did.
It crushes me like a weight I cannot lift.
I call out to you in the language of pain,
But you've forgotten the sound of my voice.

I wander through the ruins of our love,
A pilgrim searching for a god that never existed.
And every empty room whispers your name
Like a curse I cannot break.

17. The Lovers Who Never Were

We were a tragedy waiting to unfold —
A love story written in reverse.
You, the flame that never burned for me.
Me, the moth that refused to leave the fire.

I built a kingdom from my longing,
And crowned you the queen of my destruction.
You didn't ask for the throne,
But I knelt anyway, begging to be ruined.

18. The Weight of Waiting

I wait for you like night waits for dawn —
Knowing the light will never come.
I count the stars like promises you never made,
Each one a reminder of what I've lost.

My heart beats to the rhythm of hope,
A fool's drum echoing in the void.
And even as my chest collapses from the ache,
I refuse to stop waiting.

19. The Curse of Remembering

I remember you in ways I cannot forget.
Your laughter, a melody that haunts me.
Your touch, a phantom that lingers on my skin.
Your absence, a wound that never heals.

I tried to erase you from my bones,
But your name is carved into my marrow.
I carry you like a disease
I never wanted to cure.

20. The Final Goodbye I Never Gave

If I had known our last goodbye was the end,
I would have held you a little longer.
I would have memorized the weight of your hand in mine,
And the way your eyes dimmed when you looked at me.

But I let you go too easily,
Like a fool who thought love could survive distance.
Now, I spend my days grieving the moment I lost you
And my nights dreaming of the day you might return.

These verses are fragments
of a heart torn between hope
and despair. Yet, life moves
forward, as do I, even if my
words are left unspoken.

The Last Page, But Not The End

The last page of the book gently closes, but the story lingers — like a flame that refuses to fade. Maybe the words end here, but not the emotions, not the hope.

From my side, the story is far from over. I'll wait. I'll wait through the silence, through the distance, through every unanswered question and every hidden feeling. Because some chapters are worth waiting for, even if they take a lifetime to be written.

Maybe you'll never know how deeply each word was carved from my heart, or how every line whispered your name. But I'll carry this unfinished story with me, hoping that one day, you'll turn the page — and find me still there, waiting.